An unfeigned Amalgamation - A collection of Short stories

Susri Mohapatra

ISBN 978-93-5610-513-3
© Susri Mohapatra 2022
Published in India 2022 by Pencil

A brand of
One Point Six Technologies Pvt. Ltd.
123, Building J2, Shram Seva Premises,
Wadala Truck Terminal, Wadala (E)
Mumbai 400037, Maharashtra, INDIA
E connect@thepencilapp.com
W www.thepencilapp.com

Author biography

Susri Sangita Mohapatra was born in 1989 in Bhubaneswar, Odisha .Fared consistently well academically and was presented with award of excellence in Grade 10 for scoring 91.8 percentage of marks.She completed her B.Tech in Electrical Engineering and is currently working as a Manager in Consulting function of Deloitte India. She has been working as an IT professional for close to 11 years and has worked in globally renowned IT companies like Tata Consultancy Services and IBM(International Business Machine).

A techie by profession but creative at heart ;an avid reader who is passionate about wielding her avenues of imagination and transforming thoughts into words .The interest in creative writing sparked during school days which started with reading literature books and writing of essays ,articles etc as part of assignments and gradually the horizons of writing expanded beyond just the curriculum.The journey of writing had begun since then and the ecstasy of transporting the readers to a world created and envisioned by the author is definitely unparallelled...

Contact:
Email :susri_mohapatra@yahoo.com
Instagram: @mohapatra_susri
LinkedIn: Susri Mohapatra

CONTENTS

Epigraph

" Have a heart that never hardens, and a temper that never tires,
and a touch that never hurts."

-- Charles Dickens

Preface

"An Unfeigned Amalgamation - A Collection of Short Stories" is my maiden attempt in storytelling which is quite a detour from the technical arena which i dwell upon frequently.

The intent of writing this book was not just to transcend the territories of my technical space but a genuine attempt to provide the readers with the joy of reading stories that are simplistic in it's core but it's essence is substantiated by rendering a moral or message to the narrative with subtlety without preaching that I hope can be a takeaway for the readers.

~ *Susri Mohapatra*

Acknowledgements

My heartfelt gratitude goes to my family for their unconditional love and support and for being there with me through thick and thin .My literary journey would not have been possible without their indelible guidance.

I extend special thanks to my friends - *Amrita Muduli and Sagarika Satapathy*who have been instrumental in motivating and encouraging me in my literary endeavours and have always rendered me their indispensable feedback and advice.

Introduction

"An Unfeigned Amalgamation" is a collection of short stories weaved around characters that are purely fictional yet relatable.

Each story although is different in it's plot and characterisation but the common parlance are it's slice of life narrative that can be a breezy and aplomb read that caters to all generations. The youth can easily connect with the characters of the plot and I believe some might have had experiences similar to the protagonists. The very purpose of this book is to some extent enable the readers to perceive life, it's experiences ,challenges,bewilderment with a different lens and dimension.

"Dreams Fulfilled" , I believe can inspire the readers to go far and beyond in their drive and tryst of turning goals into actions and dreams into reality...

In **"The Inspiration"** , we can draw parallels with the protagonist's life as each one of us might have at some point been inspired by somebody, although the magnitude and extent of paranoia might have been heightened in it's characterisation to generate interest, but the core of the plot can definitely connect with the readers..

"The Miracle" intends to empathize the readers with the protagonist and cements one's belief in the divine superpower...

"Together Again" entails the journey of protagonists and how their love reignites after a period of lull in their journey of togetherness...

"The Wind" is an inspiring journey of gathering the courage to follow one's heart...

"The Renaissance of Love" silently and with subtlety enlightens the readers with the true meaning of love...

"The Tenderness" delves into the tender and innocent mind of a child

I hope you enjoy the stories as much as I enjoyed while writing it....

*~ **Susri Mohapatra***

The Tenderness

"Disha, please come downstairs ,baby", called out Disha's mother, Mrs. Mishra as there was a mammoth gathering in the hall downstairs. Disha swiftly came to greet the sea of people hovering around the house..

It was 15th April, Disha's birthday as she turned 7 today. Disha was beaming with happiness , her effervescent smile exuded exuberance . Her incessant chatter with innocence charmed and fascinated everybody around..She was able to capture the attention of the guests with the perennial flow of words that fluttered from her mouth which she very conveniently weaved around with stories which partly she might have read here and there and part of which was a figment of her tender imagination..She garnered praise and applause from the swarming guests for her sharp eloquence.

Disha had a penchant for telling stories. At this tender age, her art and skills of articulating the incoherent thoughts of her innocent mind amazed the listener.

As the celebration ended and the guests left, Disha without even wasting a minute started rehearsing for the elocution competition at her school tomorrow. The interschool competition was for Grade -II to V students and Disha was in Grade-II. This was her umpteenth time of practising her speech.

Disha rewound the moments of appreciation which she just received from the guests at her birthday celebration. Basking in those moments of glory, she echoed to herself in the mind that she is indeed unbeatable and the trophy is all hers. The degree and magnitude of her confidence heightened to a level that she started visualizing scenes of her going up to the stage to lift the trophy.

The next day, as she got ready for school, Mr and Mrs.Mishra checked on her if she had prepared well for the competition. Disha replied with a tinge of arrogance and left for school which startled them. Although her gestures did baffle them quite a bit but without giving much thought they presumed that the gathering and celebrations might have exhausted her .

Disha reached the school and rushed to the auditorium for the competition. The first name announced for the elocution competition was Deeshan of Grade IV. He enthralled the audience with his fluency ,confidence and articulation. The audience could not contain their excitement and gave him a standing ovation.
There were three other students- Nisha, Erica and Shobhit before Disha's name was announced. All of them were good in their own way. Watching these young talents amaze the audience with their skills was indeed a spectacle
.

Next Disha's name was announced. As she walked upto the stage of the auditorium, her mind still buoyed up to the words of praise of the last night. She took a deep sigh and started speaking her lines . She did take a few pauses here and there but overall her eloquence did manage to garner applause from the audience as well.

She was on cloud nine . Euphoric as ever, she reached home and narrated the moments of the competition to her parents with aplomb. When Mr. and Mrs.Mishra asked about other student's performance, she vehemently refused to talk about it and stated that she is the one who is going to win the competition hands down and went to her room.The glare in her eyes and her sudden overtly elevated sense of self bewildered them. Mr. and Mrs. Mishra discussed about the defiance in her attitude although it was not of much concern as it was not that overbearing or disdainful in any manner . But they did feel that the signs of change in her behavioral patterns needed to be addressed.

Disha meanwhile was ecstatic in her own wonderland. She fantasized moments of her walking up to the stage and being presented with the medal for the first prize. She reimagined those moments in her head innumerable times and then went back to sleep.

The next day she woke up and got ready for the school. Results were to be announced after 2 days. For these 2 days, she not just believed in her triumph but also started living in her world of fancy .The thoughts of victory overpowered everything else in her mind..

Finally the day of results arrived. Disha got ready for the school and it was a deja-vu moment as she once again rushed to the auditorium. The ceremony started with speeches by the esteemed jury , chief guest and the principal. All the students were deeply engrossed in listening to the words of wisdom by the esteemed panel.

Now, it was time for the results to be announced. As the name of student who bagged the first prize in elocution was about to be announced, Disha almost stood up from her seat and was about to move towards the stage, but to her surprise the name of the winner was Deeshan. Deeshan was felicitated by the jury and principal. He thanked the teachers of his class in his speech. Then the names of the second and third prize winners were announced. It was Nisha and Erica respectively. They too thanked their teachers in their speeches.

Disha was disheartened and her eyes got moist in despair. Then she heard that the panel had decided to introduce a consolation prize to encourage and motivate students who might have scored below the winners by few margins but certainly had the potential to stand out.

Disha's name was announced as the winner of the consolation prize. Disha somehow gathered herself from the setback and went up to the stage to collect her prize. She apologized for not being able to give any speech as she felt unwell. She left home immediately after the ceremony.

As she reached home with a sullen face, her parents asked her if something was wrong. She started sobbing and told them that she was not declared as the winner for the competition but was given a consolation prize. Mr. and Mr.Mishra gently consoled her and asked her to forget everything and take rest for a while. Their fear of her change in attitude was apparent now. They decided to talk to her the very next day .

It was Sunday and a holiday. They went for a stroll with her in the garden early morning ."*Look Disha, You are our world. We want nothing but the best for you..Winning and losing are a part of life. You'll win some battles and lose some as well .That's inevitable. Even if u lose , learn from your shortcomings and grow gracefully along the journey..Just make sure you put in your best foot forward everytime which you have and we appreciate that ...So, just rejoice. This is your moment*", said Mr. and Mrs. Mehera. Disha replied , "Thanks mom and dad .It means a lot".

Mr. and Mrs. Mehera decided to talk to the principal of the school the very next day if they could introduce moral science or generic counselling sessions for children as part of their curriculum and it was not just them, but several parents battling in dealing with the same issue. Simply teaching students to excel in subjects of science , history, maths isnt enough, they need to be prepared for widening their mental wavelength in dealing with the highs and lows of life as well.

Dreams Fulfilled

As Sanhvi was engrossed in framing the lines of the maiden stanza of her poem, suddenly she heard Miss. Freddy scream at her asking her to tell the mathematic formula of the Pythagoras theorem. *"Why the hell did she have to ask me now.* "she thought as she failed to answer Miss. Freddy. "Please go *out of my class.*" shouted Miss. Freddy. She stood almost embarrassed near her desk. *"Don't waste my time. Go out quickly."* Miss Freddy shouted again. Sanhvi left with her eyes moist.

After the class, her closest friend, Anay searched for her and found her in the school park sitting all alone. He rushed towards her and enquired if she was fine." *Sanhvi why don't you focus in the class. All the teachers have complaints against you. Just focus dear."* Anay told her. *"You know the reason Anay. Then why do you keep telling me this all the time."* Sanhvi reiterated. *"Okay. I lose. Let's go now else we'll miss the bus."*

They got onto the bus and sat together in the very last seat as usual and started chatting." *Anay, you know what there is an international poetry contest and I am participating in it. Poem is ready. Just have a look and give me your reviews. It should be honest right.."* Sanhvi looked at him with curiosity waiting for his reaction." *It's awesome. It doesn't require any further changes. And*

I am being completely honest. Just submit it. And I am sure you'll win the contest because there is no one better than you when it comes to imagination and bringing to life the imagined in form of words". Anay said. *"Thanks, dear. It means a lot."* Sanhvi was euphoric on hearing this.

Sanhvi was a rebel in every way and was always up to challenging the status quo. She dreamt high and was determined enough to fulfill them. She was anything but conventional. Anay on the other hand liked to always go by the rules and play safe. They were contrasting personalities and that's why both were best of friends. There was immense understanding, trust, and transparency between the two of them .

Sanhvi got down from the bus as her stop arrived. As she went inside her house, she witnessed a bunch of people hovering around discussing shares and money. *"Meet my daughter. She is in the XII th grade."* Mr. Mehera introduced Sanhvi to the guests. Mr. Mehera, Sanhvi's father was one of the eminent industrialists of the country. Sanhvi stood there listening to discussions about market position, shares, investment and after a while got so freaked out that she went into her room to relax.

As Sanhvi was about to fall asleep, her subconscious mind started visualizing scenes of her walking up the stage to collect the award for the prestigious Pulitzer prize for literature.

The next day morning, she woke up and submitted her poem for the contest and got ready for the school. Although she was present in the class, but her mind was wandering with anxiety regarding the results of the contest. She decided to vent her worry to Anay. *"Don't worry. Everything will be fine. You are a phenomenal writer."* Anay said to calm her down. *"Thanks."* Sanhvi replied with a smile.

She went home and heard some discussions between her parents planning to send her abroad for graduation and then MBA so that she could be well equipped to handle the affairs of their family business. She decided to confront her father. "*Dad, what's going on.*" "*We have planned that we'll be sending you abroad for further studies.*" Mr. Mehera replied. "*But Dad, I'm not interested in business administration. I want to get into a creative field*". Sanhvi answered." *Please don't argue . It's decided, and you'll have to abide by it. It's important for our family that you gain the necessary knowledge to handle our family business.*" Mr. Mehera was firm on his decision. Sanhvi angrily went into her room and sobbed for hours and a feeling of sheer helplessness seeped into her heart.

The XII th grade board exams got over within a month, the results were out. Sanhvi managed to score an average of just about 70 percent. Despite of that, she managed to get an admission into one of the most sought-after colleges in US. Anay was excellent in academics, he also got admission into the same college but by his own merit. Everything seemed all set and she was prepared to fly although her heart quietly desired for something else.

It was just the day before her travel date. She was just casually checking her mail. She was pleasantly surprised to receive a mail where it was mentioned that she had won the poetry contest and she was invited to join a workshop after 3 days. She was on cloud nine. Her joy knew no bounds, but her heart also ached at the same time. An avalanche of anxiety, indecisiveness and fear struck her. It was a paradoxical feeling. She decided to call Anay, who better than him could rescue her from this situation." *Can you meet me in an hour?" "Why what happened. It's so early in the morning."* Anay responded in a sleepy tone." *Don't ask any further question. Just come to the botanical park nearby my place. I'll be waiting for you there."* Sanhvi shouted. "*Okay*". Anay agreed hesitantly.

They both met at the park. Anay was sharp on time as he sensed urgency in Sanhvi's voice." *Look at this Anay. I have won the contest and I'll be felicitated in Delhi and there'll be a literary workshop in just 3 days from now.* "Sanhvi said. "*Great. Congrats but now it's too late. Tomorrow we both are supposed to fly to US. You remember."* Anay replied. "*Yeah. I know. But this was all I have always wanted, it's my dream to carve a niche for myself in the literary arena and now I am so close to it. I am planning for an escape from home without informing Mom and Dad. I'll reach Delhi by tomorrow for the felicitation."* Sanhvi said. *"What? Have you lost it?"* Anay was furious. *"It's my dream and I can't abandon it."* Sanhvi got emotional. *"But you are ready to abandon me."* Anay said.*" Abandon you. Where did this come from. Pursuing higher studies is your dream not mine. I want to pursue my own."* Sanhvi said. *"And what will be uncle and aunt's reaction when they come to know of this.And I believe there must be some other way to persuade them.."?* Anay told. *"I just don't know. I wanted you to help me in this and you are just being impossible"* Sanhvi retorted. *"Listen Sanhvi.. Is this a movie?. It's important to be practical and realistic.in life."* Anay retorted.*" "Fine. Goodbye".* Sanhvi said and left the place.

The words of Anay fluttered in the mind of Sanhvi. She realized that it was her life and her story, and she should be entitled to tell her story exactly the way she had envisioned it to be. She stood firm on her decision and planned for the escape very meticulously the next day and left a note for her parents which read.

"Lending a support to our family business isn't my dream. Going to live my dreams. Please forgive me Mom and Dad." Mr. Mehera and Mrs. Mehera were furious and tried to contact her incessantly, but her number was unreachable. They both tried to search for her in some places but couldn't track her. After a series of futile efforts, they had no choice but to succumb. Meanwhile Anay left for US for further studies.

Sanhvi was felicitated by a panel of accomplished authors worldwide. Receiving this huge honor, she felt immensely proud and humbled at the same. It was indeed a moment for her. She went back to her flat to sink in to the feeling of the glory but she felt a sense of void in her heart. She picked up her cell to call Anay, but she was reminded of the last moments of bitter conversation between the two of them, so she resisted herself. To console her inner self, she thought to herself that it was her glory and she didn't necessarily need anyone else to make her feel good.

The next day the literary workshops started in full swing. She was enthusiastic to learn and by her sheer perseverance, determination, and drive, she published 2 novels in a year both of which were bestsellers. The next year, she published poetry and that also received rave reviews and appreciation. Just within a span of 2 years she was basking in phenomenal success.

When she started to work on her third novel, she started writing lines but couldn't somehow get the feeling right. She failed to understand what was disturbing her. She stopped writing and just stared at the stars in the sky trying very hard to get over the feeling of vacuum. Almost with an uncontrollable outburst of emotions, she gathered the courage to call Anay." *Hey. How are you?*". "*Pretty good. How are you doing?*". Anay replied." *Good. Was just reminded of our good old days.*" Sanhvi said. "*Okay. I thought probably we would never be able to break the ice after what happened. Anyways congrats for all the novels, poetry that you have published. They are simply superlative.*" Anay said. "*Hmm...But I must say that I always felt this guilt within me of not having you beside me. Sorry for all that happened*" Sanhvi said with an emotional tone. Anay replied," *Well. Maybe it was meant to happen. I am sorry too coz I have realized that how passionate one can be towards one's pursuit of goals and you were right in your own way. I tried to force my views on you and judged you wrongly.* "She smiled at his reply and said," *Just leave the past. Let's meet some day. What say.*"He said," *Well, I'll be in India next month at around 15th. Let's meet then.*" "*Sure. Bye then. Catch you later.*" Sanhvi said.

They both started counting the days and waited eagerly for the 15th of next month. And then when the day arrived. Sanhvi waited for Anay's plane to land. He arrived and came waving towards her. This moment of glance suddenly melted all the anguish and pain that had piled up in their hearts. Anay accompanied Sanhvi home as she couldn't just gather the courage to face her parents. They rang the doorbell. Her mother opened the door and was dumbfounded seeing her. Meanwhile Mr.Mehera came in to check and to his surprise found Sanhvi. His heart melted. It was truly a moment of sheer togetherness...

"In the pursuit of following our dreams, we at times do tend to leave behind our loved ones and no matter how far we reach, even at the helm we tend to have a feeling of void in our heart if our journey is sans our loved ones...."

The Inspiration

The hall was filled with thunderous applause as the crowd was eagerly waiting for Sayan Sen but to their surprise, a reporter walked in. As he was about to start, the crowd was in sheer disappointment. The reporter and a well-known speaker, Karan Dsouza firstly greeted everyone with a namaste.

"Good evening ladies and gentlemen. I know that everybody gathered over here have been waiting to hear The Sayan Sen, but I would like to apologize on his behalf as he couldn't make it today due to some unavoidable circumstance. But please don't be disheartened. I know that I won't be able to make up for his absence as it's always a sheer pleasure listening to the journey of our beloved Sayan from the horse's mouth, but I promise that I won't let you down in narrating his journey. So, it's a humble request to be patient with me."

Mr. Sayan Sen, 10 novels in a span of a decade and all of them bestsellers. Today as the world is celebrating his 10 years of stupendous success in the literary field. We would all love to know his journey. What is it that inspired him into writing. Firstly, he would like to thank the people who have showered so much love and adulation on all his work. He feels extremely happy and humbled.

As a child, stories of all kind fascinated him. He was an

ardent listener and reader. During his school days, calculus didnt interest him rather every day he waited eagerly to be back from school to listen to the tales narrated by his grandparents. There was something magical in the narration that drew him to a utopian world and he was submerged in his world of imagination. Those days made him realise the power of imagination and it deeply impacted his mind and heart.

But as time passed by, the interest got buried deep under the abyss as life got in the way. The quest was still alive, but he was directionless and was almost clueless how to take it forward. Everybody in the hall listened to him with curiosity as Karan continued.

But as the great **Paulo Coelho**said, *"And ,when you want something, all the universe conspires in helping you to achieve it."*

It was the college induction, and everyone was supposed to give a brief introduction about themselves. Suddenly he heard the word 'writing' and this very word drifted his attention to the subtle voice of a girl. A blend of honesty and a hint of innocence in her voice kept him engaged as her words flew swiftly like a river as she very articulately described her passion for writing and her pursuit of it right from schooling and that she has her poetry published every month in an international magazine.

Sayan was instantly awestruck. He went back home. Something inside him triggered the dormant forces of creativity. But sadly, he couldn't hear the name of the girl.

His curiosity led him to look for her. He even enquired about her from some of his batchmates but was unable to find her. The magnitude of his inquisitiveness about her soon turned into paranoia. Why was he so obsessed with a girl whose name he didn't know, who he hadn't even seen clearly, he kept wondering. Was it just the creative connection that struck the chord in him or was it something else? The answers to it seemed like a mystery to him. After a week of mental perturbation, finally he got a sight of her. It was indeed a sight that bought a sigh of relief, a sea of serenity, and a bountiful of ecstasy back into his life.

His anxiety pushed him further into this obscure lane. He enquired her name from some of his batchmates as he couldn't gather the courage to approach her. Her name 'Sunayna Mishra' echoed in his mind. He tried very hard to recollect the name of the magazine which she had mentioned in the induction day. After thinking hard, he concluded that probably the name was," The Voice". He googled the same and found out the international magazine with the same name. He was delighted and instantly subscribed and bought a copy of the magazine. He flipped through the pages of the magazine in search of poetry by Sunayna Mishra and finally found it. As he traversed deep into the rhythms of the poem, he went through an emotional journey with a tinge of sensitivity, earnestness and meaning. The anxiety and obsession which was simmering within him for Sunayna amplified and soon transformed into adulation, adore and inspiration.

Every month he waited eagerly to read the poem by her. Her poetry not just inspired him but rendered his creative energies a definite direction. He then started to nourish and nurture his creative skills. In the college, he just got a glimpse of her, but their paths never crossed, and they never had a single conversation in the entire four years of his college life. He realised that his quest and tryst to find her made him find himself.

Post college he wielded his avenues of imagination and transformed his emotions into rhythms of poetry and thoughts and experiences into stories. He approached various publishers but faced rejections and criticisms for many years. But he worked on it constructively and was successful in building a foundation with the brickbats that were thrown at him. And well rest is history.

The audience was completely enthralled and wanted to hear more of it. One of the gentlemen from the audience asked," *Sir, it's such an amazing journey I must say. But we would love to know more of it. If you are comfortable, would you like to share what happened to the woman you said was Sayan's inspiration and did he ever get a chance to interact with her or tell her how inspired he was by her.*" Karan took a deep pause and answered," *Thank you. Well, as you guys have showered so much love. I would definitely answer that as well.*"

As I had already mentioned that Sayan didn't even speak a word with her during his college days and even during his days of struggle but the spark in her writing illuminated his creativity. Even without a spoken word and with just a few glimpses of her, he was able to feel her presence. It almost felt to him that it was a spiritual connection that bonded them, that couldn't be expressed through mere words. After few years, he was successful in his endeavour as a writer and soon became a well-known author.

One day, he was in New York to give a lecture and attend a conference. After the conference was over, he heard a familiar voice calling his name, he turned to see one of his college friends in the same room as an audience. He was thrilled," *Hi Rohan. So good to see you after a long time.* "*Yup buddy. Congratulations to you. You have truly reached heights. You made our batch proud.*" Rohan said. He further added." *Hey, did you get the marriage invitation from Sunayna, our batchmate; remember. She is getting married this week.*" He was shocked to hear this and asked." *Really. Can you just show me the invite?*". He saw the invitation and was almost choked. He immediately left the auditorium, cancelled all further meetings, and flew back to India.

Disturbed and agitated with the news, he enquired about the guy Sunayna was marrying. He used his network to get the details about the guy and found out the guy was abusive and had a past of harassing people. In a state of complete shock, he checked the venue of the wedding and rushed there instantly.

He is looking for a girl, who does not know he exists, or the story that has brought him here. He is standing near the doorway and surveying the golden banquet hall, which is filled with refined bodies in gorgeous attire, who never make facial expressions. But they will, soon. Any moment now.

He went up to the stage and opened the Pandora's box as he spoke about all the information that he had about the groom's past misconduct so that the Sunayna could be saved from the blunder. He noticed all those refined plastic guests were now in a state of shock with their eyes and mouth wide open. But Sunayna's parents threw him out of the hall as they thought it to be a cheap trick. He rebelled hard but was left with no choice but to leave the venue with a heavy heart.

This incident made him so shattered that he had almost stopped writing as he was unable to recover from the shock. Months passed by and he still couldn't move on.

One fine day, as he was engrossed in his own thoughts, he heard a knock on the door. He went and opened the door. To his surprise, he saw Sunayna. He couldn't believe it.
After marriage to the guy, Sunayna discovered that the guy was indeed all that Sayan had found out. She got separated from him. She searched for Sayan as she was intrigued by the fact that he had come all the way to her marriage to alert everybody although before that she hadn't even met him.

Sayan and Sunayna got married just few years after her separation. His inspiration is now actually his wife.
Isn't his journey as phenomenal as his writings are. The audience left the hall mesmerised.

The Miracle

The steep hilly terrain, dense evergreen forests, clouds swaying, frosty snow-clad peaks magnified the beauty of the Queen of Hills. The intense heat of the summer failed to deter the very tranquility and serenity of the summer capital, Shimla.

It was Saturday morning,29 April,2017. The Tenzin hospital was buzzing with people who had all come to take their near and dear ones back home. From Ward 17 A, Mrs. Sophie Kapoor was also getting discharged today but quite unlike the other patients, she didn't have anyone waiting for her. Mrs. Sophie Kapoor was suffering from Alzheimer's disease and was in hospital under treatment for around 15 years. Since last 5 years her health severely deteriorated and was in coma. But she started showing signs of improvement from last 1 year and today was the day when she was getting freed from the barriers of the ward but alas her intense sense of gratification remained confined to her. There was not a single close soul with whom she could share her bundles of joy barring the nurses who escorted her to her home in Kasauli .

As she stepped in, tears rolled down her cheeks as she gazed her home with wide open eyes. Abundant with feelings of ecstasy and nostalgia deep within, in an inadequacy to handle the depth of the pool of heavy emotions, suddenly she started feeling uneasy and lay on the bed for a nap.

She opened her bleary eyes ,squinting into the sunlight streaming in from the open window, traversed down the memory lane. Battling hard to gather her shattered memory, in a tryst to reminisce the moments that transpired the ghastly incident that altered the landscape of her life forever.

It was 29 May,2001."*29 May seems to be a landmark date in my life*", whispered Sophie to herself. Sophie and Akash were bitterly engaged in a battle of words. Losing her calm, she yelled at him." *Akash,today shall be the last day, of us being together. We'll be parting our ways after that. Can we not end this gracefully?*". Akash calmed down and nodded in agreement. Before Akash could say anything, she left in tears.

These memories stifled Sophie and suddenly she screamed in pain. The nurse who was present in the home as her caretaker gave her pills and she fell asleep for a while.

After some time as she regained her senses, she was submerged deep in her thoughts with umpteen questions in her mind." *Did they get separated on that fateful day? What happened after she left the place. How did she suffer from this severe medical condition ?*"She tried to recollect but her memory ceased to function beyond a point. Her quest for the answers failed miserably, her mind deserted her restless soul. The memories effaced were like some lines of a book being tampered then no matter how hard the reader apprehends to decipher, the core of the plot remains incomplete.

Taking a departure from the memories of agony and despair, she immersed herself in moments filled with euphoria

It was the first day of college in University of Information Technology , Shimla .The lectures had started and Sophie was cracking jokes and laughing aloud with her friends. The lecturer noticed and asked her to stop giggling. Akash the first bencher who was engrossed in the lecture suddenly turned back to notice the girl who caught the attention of the class. He was somehow mesmerized by the effervescence in her voice. Her exuberance struck him. His attempts to sweep her off her feet was successful and soon the Cupid's arrow struck them They both complemented each other immensely as his intensity matched with her sparkle and vivacity. Everything seemed perfect.

They decided to take their relationship to the next level. They decided to let their families know of their decision. Sophie told her parents, Mr., and Mrs. Fernandes about it and they got furious about it because of their religious and cultural differences. Akash also faced the same music. In despair after their failed attempts to convince their parents, they decided to do so without their consent. They went to a church first and then to a temple and sanctified their relationship till eternity and beyond.They went to their parents' place to seek their blessings but Sophie's parents out of sheer shock and anger disowned her. Akash's case was no different. Agitated and disturbed by recollecting the angst of her parents, Sophie rushed outside to some neighbour's place to enquire about them, she got to know that they had passed away two years back in an accident. She broke down as she learnt about it. Life could be so unfair and cruel.

After she was able to come to terms with the loss, she travelled back to the ecstatic moments of her life. The feeling of togetherness and finding peace in each other's company, their love knew no bounds. It seemed as though she was living the life she had always longed for.

But as years passed by, the feeling of vacuum struck her. She soon started realizing that she had lost her individuality and identity in a maze of romance. The ideal love, the picture-perfect marriage seemed to crumble as she battled to find her own ground. Over the years, Akash was so engrossed in his own business that he seldom could feel what she left behind to be able to build this foundation. A wide gap had creeped between them. Sophie was intensely reminded of the days with her parents where she was her chirpy, independent self. She craved for those days.

Unable to bear the burden, she erupted like a volcano one fine day. With sheer anger, she confronted him. "*Akash, do u remember when was the last time you had bothered to ask me how I have been feeling all these years? When was it when we had shared our feelings with each other? Where are those days when you could easily read my mood and could go to lengths to make me happy?*". "*We are a married couple now . We have a responsibility towards each other. We can't behave like college going guys any longer. Just be practical*" Akash retorted. "*You will never understand Akash. What has sharing feelings got to do with practicality.*" screamed Sophie. This discussion gave sleepless nights to both.

The next day, they cordially decided to work on their relationship. They made several attempts to bridge the gap by spending some evenings together, having extended conversations but no matter how hard they tried, the spark that ignited their bond earlier had somehow extinguished. The sense of detachment seemed apparent and they no longer could connect on a deeper level. The enormity of the distance that all these years that created seemed to overpower all their attempts.

"The only solution that seemed feasible at this point in time is to separate." Sophie conveyed this to Akash with a deep sigh. She was not sure if she meant it completely. Her heart pounded heavily as she uttered those words. Part of her, wished Akash to contradict her, fight with her, pursue her to give their relationship a chance and just console her. But the imagery didn't come to life as he quietly surrendered in agreement.

The incidents that followed had evaporated from her memory." *So, did we lead separate lives, or some miracle awaited to metamorphose the journey of our love*". As Sophie lay down in deep thoughts, she heard the bell ring.

The neighbour who had informed her about her parent's demise was on the door. "*Mam, there is a lean man with a beard who comes religiously to this place to enquire about a woman named Sophie. And I say him every day that no one lives here now. Today also he had come, I told him that a woman is living here from today. What's your name Mam?*" . the person asked. "*Sophie*". She replied. "*Oh. Could you please meet him Sophie Mam? He has gone for a stroll just nearby your place.*" The person said. "*Can you please tell me his name if you know*". Sophie asked. "*Sorry Mam. I don't know.* ".the person replied. "*No problem. Thanks anyways.*" she said.

She ran immediately and could faintly see a man. As she approached towards him , she put her hand on his back. He turned to see her. It was Akash. Almost speechless and dumbfounded, they looked into each other's eyes and tears rolled down. No words could describe the magnanimity of deep emotions that they felt. Sophie's quest to find the answers to the questions she was battling with no longer seemed substantial.

"Miracles do happen only if you believe in it."

Together Again

Dark swaying clouds, pearls of drizzle caressing the damp soil, the wind blowing ferociously. A blend of gentleness and aggression. The weather very aptly depicted the qualities that is indispensable to serenade the journey of life.

It was a regular weekend and Sandhya was relaxing in a coffee shop enjoying the regular sip of cappuccino. Sandhya was lost in her contours of imagination very deeply delving into the weather depicting life's philosophy. Well, as she was engrossed in her wandering thoughts, suddenly the cacophony of the ring of her cell phone distracted her and she very unwillingly surrendered to attending the call.

" *Hey Sandhya. How is life? Long Time How is Vinay dear. Just called you to invite you and Vinay to our college get- together. It's on 2nd May. Just 15 days to go. Will be fun. You both made such a wonderful couple. Everybody would be excited to see you both*". I was about to say "*Look Meera*", without even listening, she hung up saying "*got to go. Bye. See you then*". "*Bye Meera*". She was such a chatter box. She kept on speaking without even giving Sandhya an opportunity to utter a word or give any sort of explanation. But that's the way she had always been.

Sandhya traversed down the lanes of the past. The pages of love brought back memories of ecstasy, passion, angst, all battling together. Well the mixed bag of emotions as they say the journey of love brings.

It was the first day in college. Nervousness, Anxiousness, Curiosity, Uncertainty, Excitement. All these feelings flowing like a river. After the introduction class, physics classes started. As the lecturer explained Electromagnetic theory and it's effects, suddenly a baritone voice was heard questioning the lecturer and the lecturer was struggling to justify to the volley of questions thrown at him. The guy's confidence and courage somehow startled me as to how he picked up an argument with the lecturer on the very first day while the only thing I could hardly do on the first day was to nod to whatever the lecturer explained. Well, this was the first impression that I had of Sameer. Very outspoken and confident.

The scenario after the lecture was worth a vision. All the girls suddenly surrounded this guy almost in a tryst to grab his attention. Well, what a flirtatious character he must be, Sandhya thought and without even giving a damn to this group chatter left to the library. Within minutes her eyes and mind started wandering here and there and she noticed the ladies' man in the library and what a nuisance he looked around and sat next to her. She pretended to study some heavy topics without even understanding an iota of it and noticed that he tried hard to somehow strike a conversation with her but she seemed quite uninterested and replied with just a '*Hmm*'or a '*Yeah*'. After few minutes, they both left the library with an awkward silence.

Then they started meeting very often and her shackles of judgement about him soon started to fade away and when this awkward silence transformed to sheer togetherness, she had no clue. Day after day the buds of love blossomed. And then finally, it was the day of marriage, of commitment, of promises. The air was filled with eternal and divine happiness. She wished she could turn back the clock and bring the wheels of time to a stop.

Initially it was as if heavenly love bestowed upon them. After few years Samaira was born to them. As days passed, reality thrust upon them and opened a Pandora's box. Soon they started fighting over petty issues. Sandhya felt like walking alone in this journey. He bought his work juggles into the table and she bought her loneliness. A wide gap was created between them which seemed almost impossible to bridge. They were living together but their hearts and mind were no longer together. The fire that ignited had extinguished. One fine day, she decided to move away instead to living a life of pretense.

Since then it's been almost four years, they have been living separately. Sandhya started working as a banker since then and had created her own small little world. Samaira truly makes her feel complete.

Suddenly, she heard a shrilling voice "Mama" and she turned around to see her beautiful daughter running towards her. To her surprise, she saw Sameer behind her." *Look who is here*". Sandhya was startled and dumbfounded, didn't know what to say and simply smiled. Then she left to play with her friends. As Sameer sat down in front of her, they possibly didn't have anything to say. She wondered how time and circumstances change the equation between people.

"Hey, how are you". As Sameer asked.,she thought did it really matter to him or did he even ever bother about that over the last few years. Anyways there was no point in getting into that, so just smiled, and said *"Good"*. "I have come here for a conference and will be in Mumbai for about a month. Will meet you tomorrow. Is that fine. *"Yes. Of course."* Sandhya said. Well, why does he have to meet me. Meeting could ignite feelings and emotions with some past baggage that could possibly unfold moments good or bad. Baffled and almost muddled she left the place. The night before she had feelings of nostalgia. What if meetings would trigger moments of weakness and they would fall prey to their emotions. Well, it's better not to presume things before it's occurrence and she went back to sleep.

The next day, Sandhya completed her daily chores and made Samaira ready for school. Her endearing smile propelled her to harness energy and strength that could sail her through the day. The doorbell rang and she saw Sameer outside. Sandhya asked him to come in. He bid goodbye to Samaira as she left.

"*Would you like to have some tea or coffee*". she asked and then went to the kitchen. He was in the hall seemed quite nervous and tensed. Sandhya came back and they together had a sip of coffee. It had been years since they had this moment of togetherness. "*Well, the coffee is really good*", he smiled. She replied with "*Thanks*". At least he appreciated Sandhya thought and then again juggled with thoughts that must have said out of courtesy.

Then he asked about her work to break the ice. She sensed that he wanted to say something but was somehow holding himself back. ,"*I have a conference in an hour. Got to go. Will catch up tomorrow again this time*".Sameer said "*Sure*". Sandhya replied.
I wondered again what is it that he was trying to say. With an ocean of thoughts and assumptions in my head, I got up to prepare lunch for Samaira as it was time for her to be back.

Sandhya didn't think she would ever fall in love again."*I know that everyone says that after a heartbreak, but the difference is that I'm not heartbroken. I'm not cynical, or pessimistic, or sad. I honestly believed I would never have that love again. But... then life is long. And I'm feeling things right now that I haven't in a long, time.*" she thought.

The sudden emergence of Sameer in her life ignited feelings in her heart that she had buried long back and its resurgence almost seemed impossible. But life never ceases to surprise us.

Sameer and Sandhya started meeting very often. Feelings of love, longingness, passion renewed. Sandhya could see the same in his eyes as well. She battled hard with her inner self to bottle all those feelings and not allow it to flourish so that she no longer treaded on the path of broken love and shattered heart. Out of sheer fear and angst, Sandhya told him, *"Sameer I think, we shouldn't be meeting further. It isn't just feeling right. Let's face it. Our paths can never be the same again."*

"Yeah I know that but all these days that I spent with you ,are some of the most memorable days of my life. After connecting with you again, I realized what I had missed all these years." Sameer said..*"Sameer these things don't make any sense right now. Let's just be pragmatic."*Sandhya retorted.. *"Okay. But could you please agree to my request. Tomorrow is our college reunion. Can we just go there together,"*Sameer said. *"No. It's not possible at all. I just can't put up a pretense.* "Sandhya replied. Sameer held her hand and said." *Please Just one last time. Please...".* Sandhya agreed.

The next day she woke up and went across the window. Suddenly the warmth of the sun rays struck her, the wind blew and in a sudden whiff evaporated all the baggage that she had carried for so long. It just felt so light. Immersed in the gamut of thoughts, what was it about the day that instilled a sudden wave of positive emotions within her, suddenly she heard her phone ringing." *Hello, Sandhya. Please be ready. Will reach by 10 AM."* Sameer had called.

Sandhya wore a red gown which was the first anniversary gift from Sameer. The emotional value of the dress made her nostalgic and she traversed down the memory lane reminiscing her first anniversary. As she was lost in the thoughts, the doorbell rang. As she opened the door, it was Sameer..

As they reached the venue, it felt so amazing being around old friends and the conversations amongst them made her revisit all those good old fun moments. Meera one of our common friends announced *"Sameer and Sandhya, our batch's most lovable and popular couple, wouldn't it be great guys if they share their beautiful journey with us. Let's hear it from them guys."* Sandhya was reluctant and tried to stop Meera to make the announcement, but she didn't. Sameer held my hand and narrated with a poetic zest in his voice. I could see love in his eyes after a long time. At the end, I had tears in my eyes. We received a thunderous applause from everybody...

Little did they apprehend that this reunion would lead to an absolute metamorphosis in their lives.

"Life is so curiously capricious and she realized that people who are meant to be together will always find a way back. They may take a few detours, but they are never lost in the journey of life..."

The Wind

The stage is set. The curtains have risen. Hysteria amongst the crowds seems unparalleled as Rishaan entered the arena as Landen Carter of *"A walk to remember"* .Cheers, Applause, standing ovation. The Reaction just seemed overwhelming. He felt the world was at his feet...

Suddenly the alarm bell rang. Oh it was a dream he realised. Rishaan had always been passionate about the stage, performing and bringing smiles on the faces of millions of onlookers .All of a sudden, a feeling of nostalgia took over almost like a thunderstorm. He recollected the days when his life revolved around drama, art and the joy of performing and how the love of his life was witness to all those incredible moments. Before he could be completely seeped in the feeling of melancholy of losing both the pillars of his life, his performing instincts and the love of his life, Meera, he was horrified being late to the dreary meeting in office .

He rushed from bed to get ready and reached office. Yes, he willingly or unwillingly ,rightly or wrongly worked in one of the country's top IT firm. His presentation of the design before the client wasn't satisfactory and was asked for a design change due to some inappropriate coding standards. Completely messed up and exhausted ,took a half day leave and left for the home. Rested for a while and checked his mails ,was pleasantly surprised to read the wedding invitation card of one of his closest friend, Tara. Tara was Meera's friend .She was the mediator who brought Rishaan and Meera together. He was so glad that he immediately called her up and congratulated her. He wanted to somehow ask about Meera's whereabouts but something within him resisted and shied away .He tried to make excuses for not being able to make it to the wedding because he didn't wish to gather the pieces that were left some years back but her constant insistence made him agree .

A complete paradoxical feeling choked him. Glad yet hesitant .Glad that the wedding would be a reunion of sorts , hesitant of facing the consequences of an encounter with an ex lover .A week passed with the monotony of office life. Finally the day arrived .

It was still dawn when Rishaan stepped out of the cab and walked towards the entry gate of the Delhi airport. The early morning air was pleasantly cold.

He was travelling to Bengaluru. This wedding was also going to be a reunion of his batchmates. But what he didn't know was that the reunion would begin much ahead of time; right in the queue in front of the airline counter.

He was almost sure it was she. Curiosity had his eyes glued to her. And then about 60-odd seconds later, when she turned, she proved him right. His ex-girlfriend stood two places ahead of him in that queue. They had never met after the college farewell. They walked past each other as if completely oblivious of each other's presence .Her seat was two rows ahead of him. He tried looking at her from behind .

As the flight took off , he went down the memory lane, recollecting by far some of the most heartfelt memories of his life.

It was the second year of graduation in the National Institute of Technology and Mr.Swaminathan was teaching about the Maxwell's equation of Electromagnetic theory and Rishaan was lost wandering about the equation of Jamie Sullivan and Landen Carter of Nicholas Sparks '*A walk to remember*' and how to bring to life these characters in his play in the college fest. Suddenly he heard a sharp voice asking for permission to enter the hall, Mr.Swaminathan almost surprised and asked for her introduction and informed her that it was the second year lecture and the 1st year lecture was downstairs. She apologised and moved out. Those two minutes he watched her and was somehow struck by the confidence and flair in her voice.

As the lecture was over, he rushed to the auditorium for auditioning for the female character in his play .To his surprise, he saw the same girl whose voice had an impact on him and he was wrong, it wasn't just the voice ,it was also her expressions that left him dumbfounded. Quite unanimously she was selected to play Jamie Sullivan opposite Rishaan .

"*Our love is like the wind .I can't see it but I can feel it*". While enacting the character on stage, the wind of love actually struck him. The play was an instant hit amongst the students of the campus .

The entire night ,Rishaan's mind, heart and soul was drenched with her thoughts. The next day he somehow went to her to express what he felt for her ,looking at her eyes he could feel the love for him also .He wished that moment never passed and thereafter he rewound and played that moment in his mind for the umpteenth time to keep it alive in his heart .

The announcement of flight landing was made and Rishaan came out from his world of dreams .They walked out of the flight without really acknowledging each other .He saw her looking for a taxi. He had found one and offered her to sit in it. After some time they exchanged smiles with a cordial *"Hi"* and then silence invaded between them .

They reached the venue. Tara had sent some of her relatives to escort them to the resort. It was a grand resort .From halls to decoration ,everything seemed larger than life.

They finally met Tara and congratulated her .She looked blatantly confused seeing them together but Meera instantly cleared the confusion citing it as a coincidence.

The would-be bride made them meet the whole gang of friends who had arrived little earlier than them.After a really long time, the entire batch was together again. There was noise, chaos ,laughter ,banter .It felt time had cycled back again to those days of joy and togetherness.

It was evening and Rishaan went for a stroll in the park in front of the resort and noticed Meera sitting on a bench .He looked at her and traversed down the lane of nostalgia .All those moments of their love and togetherness started haunting him.

It was the end of final year of graduation and Rishaan was still in search of a job. Most of the companies that came for recruitment to the college had rejected him .Meera was about to join a reputed company and her family was looking for a suitable guy for her to settle down. She insisted him to talk to her family about their relationship but he did try to explain it to her that his current state wouldn't permit him to face them That created a tiff between them and this tiff created a distance that could never be bridged.

Neither did he have a job to be financially secure nor he was able to express before his parents that his real passion wasn't in software and engineering rather it was drama and arts .To make things even worse he lost Meera too. He felt as if trapped in a labyrinth not knowing the way out of this embroil .Suddenly he heard a noise and came out of his flashback mode and went near Meera to break the ice.

He started with a casual conversation and then cracked some jokes to lighten up the atmosphere .As she laughed he looked at her and could feel the flames of love illuminating his heart all over again .

As they met, with every single day, his longing for her increased by leaps and bounds.
He decided to propose her again on the wedding day so that the dormant piece of his heart gained senses all over again.

It was the wedding day. Very nervously he decided to go to her after several rehearsals, but was kind of in a state of shock to see a well built and sophisticated looking guy chatting with her. With curiosity, he enquired about him from Tara and got to know that he was Meera's fiance .Rishaan was completely shattered from within .His world came to a standstill as he lost her once again. The pain and agony of losing her again stifled him from within and the very next morning, he abruptly left the place without informing anyone .
After reaching, he apologised to Tara but she could very well understand his pain. After days of drudgery at workplace coupled with the melancholy of losing the love of his life, it suddenly struck him the significance of having the courage to follow one's heart

"The ocean of life is meticulously driven by the tide of courage of following the desire of heart".

The very next day ,he quit his job and let his heart out before his parents about his passion of drama and arts .

After a year of rigorous training and preparation ,he started performing in plays and shows. He was living his dream. The gratification was unparalleled. He might have lost Meera but could feel her presence and essence still in his life

"Love is like the wind.. One can't see it but can feel it."

Renaissance of Love

Dark clouds swaying ,rainbow like a kaleidoscope of colours in the sky. The picturesque landscape in Darjeeling perfectly resonated and romanticised the gamut of emotions experienced by Aman and Kiara.

As they both walked hand in hand, his cell rang. A familiar voice said *"Hello. Diya here"*. Aman was shocked and after a long sigh replied with a *"Hello"*. He went down the memory lane and reminisced the memories that transpired his relationship with Kiara.

It was the first day of Aman in one of the country's premier institutions. The hustle bustle of the madding crowd in the college premise made him terribly nervous. Amidst the pandemonium ,he somehow gathered courage and asked one of the students,Kiara the direction for English lectures. Kiara was someone who was fiercely confident and spoke her mind .

Kiara instantly befriended Aman and made the somewhat timid Aman comfortable within seconds Aman had found a confidant in Kiara. Their friendship groomed and very soon they turned out to be an indispensable part in each other's lives.

Gradually Kiara's realised that their connection was more than just mere friendship. Kiara never knew how to bottle up her feeling. So, she expressed the same to Aman .Aman on the other hand was pretty apprehensive about the same and her words left him baffled .Silence invaded between the two for the first time. Myriad thoughts conquered his mind. Kiara was a special friend but he wasn't very sure of the love equation that was in question. As someone who never spoke his mind, he agreed to Kiara's proposal as even in his distant thought, he would never think of hurting her feelings or disappoint her in any which way.

Soon their friendship blossomed into something deeper and substantial. Aman felt secure in her company. Although he felt stable, but at times longed for that magic spark of love that he felt somehow missing in their relationship. That vacuum made him restless at times but never expressed. A year passed in each other's company. Everything just seemed perfect.

One fine morning as Aman was sipping coffee at his place little did he expect fate would take a different course altogether. The bell rang ,his parents along with their family friends arrived. He was introduced to Diya the lovely daughter of his parents' friend. Aman was awestruck for a while. As Diya spoke ,her eyes expressed volumes and he seemed quite fascinated by her.. Even after Diya left , his heart and mind were ablaze by her words, her voice and her captivating beauty.

As he woke up the next day, he noticed missed calls from

Kiara. He didn't seem to care as his mind had completely surrendered to the thoughts of Diya He bunked college for few days and ignored Kiara's calls .

Kiara was terribly worried and rushed to his place and found him lying on his bed. She decided to confront him. There was an exchange of fire between them. Aman made excuses of bad headache the reason. Kiara although calmed down momentarily but her heart could feel that there was a bigger reason than this. The next few days seemed normal. They spent time together but Aman seemed visibly lost. Kiara could feel that he was physically present with her but mentally something else was going on within him. As days passed although together, they grew emotionally distant from each other. Kiara was mentally agitated with his sudden changing behavioral pattern. Aman on the other hand seemed unperturbed by Kiara's state of mind rather his mind was still occupied with the thoughts of this sudden newfound attraction that he felt.

Kiara felt may be a change from the regular monotony could render their relationship a spark all over again. She decided to go on a trip to Darjeeling with Aman. Aman agreed thinking may be a change of place might help him also recover from the thoughts of the mystery girl.

As they boarded the flight , he was pleasantly surprised to find Diya in the same flight and row as he and Kiara. Kiara fell asleep in the flight. In the middle of the flight, she woke up to go to the washroom. When she returned she was too lazy to push her way into the middle seat. And with Aman readily offering to shift seats , the seating arrangement changed. With 30 mins still remaining for the flight to land ,a sleep starved Kiara took a power nap holding Aman's right hand firmly. Aman on the other hand nervously tried to strike a conversation with Diya. Diya's heart skipped a beat and she didnt answer pretending to have not heard Aman.The changing behavioral dynamics between the three perhaps gave a foreboding of what was to come in Darjeeling.

When the flight landed at the airport, Aman felt uncanny, his excitement seemed replaced by an unknown fear that he found very difficult to decipher. Aman followed Diya clueless of the repercussions and expressed all that he felt for her since past few days. This scene left Kiara in a state of shock. Filled with anguish and despair, she left the place. Aman felt trapped in a labyrinth unable to discover the way out from this emotional muddle. He discussed his attraction towards Diya with Kiara which she found hard to bear and left the place immediately in tears leaving Aman to choose between the two of them.

Soon Aman proposed Diya .Diya was ecstatic but Aman was batting with the guilt of not being able to keep up the trust of his closest friend. After few weeks passed a longing for genuine warmth seeped in his heart. He missed and reminisced his moments with Kiara, how she instantly understood his words that were unexpressed, how she was a guiding light for him in all his dark moments, how she stood by him firm at times when he was shaken. He realised that she completed him and the magical spark that he was longing for was actually Kiara which he never realised when she was around him. He remembered the moments of laughter of joys of misunderstanding of togetherness. Every valuable moment that he could ask for was with Kiara. He realised that true love transcends all the superficiality and it's about living and growing with each other .

He dropped a note to Diya and left immediately to meet Kiara hoping to get her back. He met her and apologised to her with a promise of being with her regardless of any circumstances .Kiara certainly didnt agree to his insistence and further stated that she was supposed to leave abroad for higher studies the very next day. Aman was left alone disheartened.

"True love is looking beyond the apparent and rising and growing each day with the person you love...".

Afterword

This book is a conglomeration of short stories that encapsulates journeys of characters etched quite diverse in disposition yet are relatable,believable and congenial.
The protagonists have depth in their emotions, are flawed to some extent, make mistakes like most of us do and own them . The women characters depicted in the stories are a powerhouse of strength, ambition and very much believe in living life on their own terms. The aberration in the characters have been dealt with subtlety without a tone of condemnation or judgement. The rendition of each short story is substantiated with a moral or message that the reader can imbibe.

In the journey of life ,we all experience highs and lows, are victims of circumstances, make blunders along the way but instead of being harsh and resentful about it , we need to learn and grow from the experiences.
The very purpose of this book is to provide the readers with not just an experience of joy but also to instill some meaningful lessons of life .....

~ Susri Mohapatra

Glossary

Pythagoras theorem: Pythagorean theorem, the well-known geometric theorem that the sum of the squares on the legs of a right triangle is equal to the square on the hypotenuse

Queen of Hills: Shimla is popularly known as the queen of hills that spread across seven hills in the northwest Himalayas

Electromagnetic theory:Electromagnetic theory based on Maxwell's equations establishes the basic principle of electrical and electronic circuits over the entire frequency spectrum from dc to optics.

A walk to remember:A Walk to Remember is a novel by American writer Nicholas Sparks, released in October 1999. The novel,,is a story of two teenagers who fall in love with each other despite the disparity of their personalities.A Walk to Remember is adapted in the film of the same name

www.ingramcontent.com/pod-product-compliance
Lightning Source LLC
La Vergne TN
LVHW050420160726
843469LV00041B/1164

9 789356 105133